SNOW-MAN STONE AGE

By Tommy Donbavand
& Steve Beckett

TITLES IN THE SNOW-MAN SET

HOT HOT HOT!
WINDY POPS!
STONE AGE
IT'S A GAS!
WHAT A DRIP!
COLD FRONT

**Badger Publishing Limited
Oldmedow Road,
Hardwick Industrial Estate,
King's Lynn PE30 4JJ**

Telephone: 01438 791037
www.badgerlearning.co.uk

2 4 6 8 10 9 7 5 3 1

Stone Age
ISBN 978-1-78464-353-9

Publisher: Susan Ross
Senior Editor: Danny Pearson
Editorial Coordinator: Claire Morgan
Illustration: Steve Beckett
Designer: Fiona Grant

STONE AGE

CONTENTS

Cole Day lives in the town of Shiverton with his parents, his sister, Winter, and pet dog, Jeff.

All a bit boring until, one day... **COSSSSHHH!** A stray snowball hit Cole on the back of his head!

But it wasn't just any snowball. It was a RADIOACTIVE snowball! And it turned Cole into Snow-Man – the world's chilliest superhero!

Now, whenever he munches on a raw carrot, Cole's body transforms into a big, white, fluffy man of action!

It's down to Snow-Man and his team, **THIN ICE** and **FROSTBITE**, to defeat the world's nastiest weather-changing villains.

Bad guys, you'd better freeze! SNOW-MAN is slip-sliding your way...

CAST OF CHARACTERS

Cole

Winter

Jeff

Hayley Stone

SNOW-MAN

VOCABULARY

admitted   mechanic
cautiously   staggered
hailstone   tightened

Chapter One

Grit

Cole Day selected the correct sized spanner from his dad's tool box and tightened the final wheel of his new go-kart.

Wiping the oil from his hands, he stood back to admire his work.

"Looking good!" he said. "I'm bound to win the Shiverton *Roll Down The Hill A Bit Race* this afternoon."

His sister, Winter, said: "Hmmm…"

Cole turned to look at her. "What does 'Hmmm…' mean?"

"Well," said Winter. "Don't you think it's a bit… small?"

Cole studied the vehicle again. He had built it all by hand from pieces of wood he had found in the garage and the wheels from his sister's old toy pram.

"It may be slightly on the 'compact' side," he admitted. "But that just means it will go faster."

Winter frowned. "How does that work?"

"I don't know!" said Cole. "But I'm sure it will all look better once I've given it a coat of paint."

Jeff, Cole's trusty dog, padded over with a paintbrush in his mouth – just as Mum arrived. She was carrying a glass of something dark and green.

"How's my little mechanic?" she asked, ruffling Cole's hair.

"Not too bad, thanks," Cole said. He eyed the glass of green stuff nervously. "What's that?"

"It's an energy shake," said Mum brightly. "I invented it myself."

"What's in it?" asked Winter.

"Everything that's green and good for you!" said Mum.

"Spinach, apple, broccoli..."

"That sounds nice," said Cole.

"...and grass," Mum finished.

Cole blinked. "Grass?"

"Loads of it," Mum grinned. "From our very own garden, too!"

"You mean the same garden where Jeff goes when he needs the loo?"

"That's the one!" Mum said. "Now, who wants a taste?"

Jeff ran and hid in the corner.

"We'd love to try it Mum," said Cole, "but Winter and I are just heading out to take my new go-kart for a test drive."

"I thought you wanted to paint it first..." said Winter.

"Nope!" said Cole. Then he pushed his go-kart out into the street as quickly as he could.

Chapter Two
Pebble

Outside, Cole sat in his new go-kart for the first time.

His throat rested on his knees, and he had to reach around his thighs to grip the steering rope.

"OK," he gurgled. "It might be a bit on the small side…"

"A bit?" scoffed Winter. "It's like you made it with an ant in mind!"

WHEEEEE! SMASH!

Cole stared at his sister. "What did you make those noises for?"

"What noises?" asked Winter. "I didn't make any noises."

"Yes you did," said Cole. "After you'd finished speaking, you said "*WHEEEEE! SMASH!*""

"That wasn't me!"

"Then what was it?"

WHEEEEE! SMASH!

The sound came again only, this time, it was accompanied by a huge ball of ice that struck the ground right in front of Cole's go-kart, leaving a hole in the pavement.

"Wow!" said Winter, picking up the frozen sphere. "That's a HUGE hailstone!"

WHEEEEE!

SMASH!

Within seconds, dozens of similar huge hailstones were hammering down from the sky – leaving big dents in cars, breaking windows, and giving passing shoppers a headache they wouldn't forget in a very long time.

Giant hailstones continued to fall all around them.

"Quick!" cried Winter. "Let's get back indoors!" She began to push the undersized go-kart back towards the garage doors.

"Not without finding out who's behind this!" said Cole, using his heels as a brake.

"I'll tell you who's behind all this!" cried a voice.

Cole and Winter spun around to find a young girl standing behind them.

She was dressed in a blue and yellow super-suit and carrying what looked like a toy space gun.

It was shiny red, and covered with flashing lights, thick wires, switches and dials.

"I know you!" said Cole, jumping out of his go-kart's seat.

"You're **Hayley Stone** – the smallest girl in town."

"No one will laugh at me for being small now that I have my Grow-Gun!" laughed Hayley.

She aimed her weapon up to the nearest cloud and fired.

Instantly, huge hailstones hammered down from the sky, smashing into everything in sight.

WHEEEEE! SMASH!

WHEEEEE! SMASH!

"OK," said Cole urgently. "I think it may be carrot time!"

Chapter Three

Stone

Back inside the covered garage, Cole pulled a raw carrot from his pocket and took a huge bite.

Instantly, a frozen whirlwind blew up from the floor next to the go-kart and wrapped itself around the trio. Icicles flashed, rain showered and snow settled at their feet.

A moment later - exactly where Cole had been – stood a white giant of a figure, dressed in a top hat and red scarf.

He had eyes as black as coal, and what remained of the carrot formed his nose.

This was SNOW-MAN - the world's chilliest superhero!

Standing beside Snow-Man were the two members of his super team – a young girl named Thin Ice, and Frostbite – a dog with a paintbrush clamped in his teeth.

"OK," said Snow-Man, striking a heroic pose. Water drops landed around his feet. "It's spring, and not quite as cold as when I'm usually needed. Let's make this fast!"

"It's Hayley Stone," explained Thin Ice. "She's got some sort of wacky weapon she's using to increase the size of ice crystals in the clouds."

"That sounds complicated," Snow-Man admitted.

"It probably is," said Thin Ice, "but the end result is giant hailstones falling to Earth and smashing everything in sight!"

"But why?"

"Why what?"

"Villains may not be smartest ice cubes in the tray," said Snow-Man, "but even they usually have a reason for their wicked schemes."

"So, you want to go out there in the middle of a killer hailstorm and ask the bad girl what's upsetting her?"

"That's the plan!" Snow-Man grinned.

"But, all it needs is one CLONK on the head from a huge hailstone and you'll be out cold!" Thin Ice pointed out.

Snow-Man thought for a second. "Then it sounds like I'll need some kind of protective hat..."

Chapter Four
Rock

Cautiously, Snow-Man stepped out of the garage wearing Dad's metal toolbox on his head.

Large hailstones continued to batter the ground all around him – and some even hit the home-made helmet with a clatter.

WHEEEEE! TONK!

WHEEEEE! TONK!

Thin Ice and Frostbite crept along behind their boss, trying to stay in his snowy shadow to avoid being hit.

Eventually, the trio were close enough to Hayley Stone to shout to her above the noise of the storm.

"Hayley!" bellowed Snow-Man. "Why are you doing this? Is it because you're so small that everyone in Shiverton points and laughs at you – if they can even see you, that is?"

Hayley Stone glared at the hero's frozen features. "What did you say?"

"Oh, didn't you know?" continued Snow-Man. "People call you names because you're so tiny and small…"

"What kind of names?" screamed Hayley.

Snow-Man shrugged. "Names like Pimple Head, Titchy Toes, The Minuscule Madam, and so on…"

Hayley Stone looked as though she was going to explode with rage.

Thin Ice pulled at Snow-Man's scarf. "Do you really think you should be saying all this?" she hissed.

But Snow-Man didn't seem to hear her. Instead, he continued his shouting conversation with the undersized villain.

"Do those names upset you?" he asked.

"Of course they upset me!" roared Hayley. "And that's why I'm going to use my giant hailstones to destroy Shiverton! Then my parents will have to move to a different town where – hopefully – I'll only be the second-smallest person!"

Snow-Man frowned. "What, you think there's a town somewhere with a person even smaller than you? I doubt it, Little Legs!"

Frostbite was quickly at his master's side. "*BARK! WOOF! GROWL!*" he said.

"Yes, I know, Frostbite," said Snow-Man. "I know she's about to snap and shoot me with her Grow-Gun, and that's exactly what I want her to do."

"It is?" whispered Thin Ice.

Snow-Man raised himself up to his full height and glared down at Hayley Stone. "Do your worst, Pixie Pants!"

Chapter Five

Boulder

The blast from the Grow-Gun hit Snow-Man full in the chest.

The chilly hero staggered back a few metres, the toolbox falling off his head – and then he began to grow.

Within seconds he was as tall as the trees, then the houses, and finally his head reached up into the cold, grey clouds.

"Perfect!" he bellowed in a voice like thunder.

"Hayley Stone can't supersize her lumps of ice if there aren't any left!"

Snow-Man took a deep breath and blew as hard as he could against the clouds. They whizzed away across the sky, leaving Shiverton forever at top speed and leaving behind a clear sky and bright sun.

"Where will they stop?" cried Thin Ice.

Snow-Man peered towards the horizon, searching for the cloudy culprits. "They've gone all the way to Little Shiverton," he said. "And now, I can use the heat of the sun to shrink me back down to size…"

As Snow-Man began to melt back to normal, Hayley slumped to the pavement. "I'm still the smallest girl in Shiverton!" she sobbed.

"Not if we can help it," said Thin Ice kindly. She took the Grow-Gun from the villain and gave her a tiny blast. Not much – just enough so that she grew a few inches in height.

"My super-suit is a bit tight now," she said, looking down at her new, taller self. "I'll have to go shopping for clothes."

"And for material to help fix all the big holes you made all over town," Snow-Man reminded her.

Hayley Stone nodded. "You're right," she said. "I'll use my pocket money to pay for my wrong-doings."

Frostbite snatched up the Grow-Gun in his teeth.

"I suppose we'd better go and destroy this thing," said Snow-Man.

Thin Ice took it from the dog's grip and smiled.

"Maybe we could just use it once more before that," she smiled. "After all – Cole will need a slightly bigger go-kart if he's to win this afternoon's *Roll Down The Hill A Bit Race*!"

QUESTIONS

1. What did Cole build for the race? *(page 6)*

2. What colour were the ingredients in Mum's smoothie? *(page 8)*

3. What did the villain bring smashing down from the sky? *(page 11)*

4. How did she make these things so large? *(page 14)*

5. Which character grew very tall? *(page 23)*

6. How did Snow-Man get rid of the clouds? *(page 26)*

MEET THE
AUTHOR AND ILLUSTRATOR

THE AUTHOR

Tommy Donbavand spent his school days writing stories in which more popular kids than him were attacked and devoured by slavering monsters. Years later, he's still doing the same thing – only now people pay him for it. The fools!

THE ILLUSTRATOR

Steve Beckett has a robot arm that is programmed to draw funny pictures. He likes playing with toy soldiers and dreams of being an ace survival expert. He is scared of heights, creepy crawlies and doesn't like camping!